The Legend of DIRTY BERT the BANDIT

WANTED

DIRTY BERT
REWARD
$50·00

Written by Marcia Vaughan

Illustrated by David Roberts

Chapter 1

From the day Bert was born he was a gritty, grimy, grubby little boy.

Everything about Bert was dirty. His clothes were dirty. His toes were dirty. Even the freckles on his nose were dirty.

His mother threw up her hands. "Bert, you're so dirty you make the pigs look clean!"

"*Dooty Buurt*," he giggled with glee. And the name stuck like mud.

Being covered with all that muck didn't slow Bert down a bit. He could run fast as lightning. Which is just what he did at bath time.

"Come back, Bert," his mother would call. "You don't want to be a stinky little skunk, do you?"

"Stinky little skunk," sang Bert as he skipped out of sight.

As the years went by, Bert became dirtier and dirtier. By the time he grew up, Bert was dirtier than dirt itself. As a matter of fact, it was hard to tell where all that dirt stopped and Bert began.

4

Although Bert was a clever fellow, he found there were few jobs for a man of his talents. He could make fleas flee, skunks cry and pull stuck pigs out of the mud better than anyone. Yet for some strange reason nobody wanted to hire him.

So Dirty Bert became a bandit.

In those days there was no shortage of big, bad bandits roaming the Wild West: Pick-Pocket Pete, Light-Fingers Lil and Snitcher the Kid, just to name a few. These bandits holed up in No-Name Cave and rode out together robbing trains, banks and stagecoaches, scaring the daylights out of the general public.

There was no meaner bunch of bandits anywhere around
until the day Bert swaggered up to their secret hideout.

"What's that stink?" shouted Pick-Pocket Pete.

"Ain't it about time you washed those socks of yours, cowboy?" Light-Fingers Lil asked Snitcher the Kid.

"It's not me," the Kid cried, pointing a finger at the newcomer. "It's him!"

The robbers threw up their hands and sank to their knees. "We surrender!" They gasped. They gagged. They begged for mercy.

"You can put your hands down. I'm a rooting-tooting, money-looting bandit just like you," Bert bragged, flicking the flies away from his face. "And I've come to join . . ."

Before he could even finish, the bandits leapt on their horses and rode for the hills. Bert wiped his dirty nose on his dirty sleeve. "I reckon I'd rather rob alone anyway," he said.

Suddenly he caught sight of something standing in the shadows of the cave. "A horse!" he grinned. "I guess those bandits won't mind if I borrow this old nag for a while."

Bert dragged the horse outside and hauled his smelly self up into the saddle. With a snort the old nag caught a noseful of Bert. It swayed to the right; it swayed to the left. Kerplop! It dropped to the dirt in a dead faint.

Bert let out a long sigh. "Reckon I'd just as soon walk."

Chapter 2

So Dirty Bert went about the business of being a bandit all alone.

His speciality was holding up stagecoaches. Bert's plan was simple. He had only to stand in the road, raise his arms and wait. One whiff of this rotten rascal made the horses faint, the driver choke and the guard swoon.

The passengers would hold their noses and shout to Dirty Bert, "PHEW! You stink worse than a bear's breath, worse than pond scum, worse than an old dry cow pie!"

And they'd throw their money and jewels at him just to make him go away.

In no time at all Dirty Bert became the most feared bandit the Wild West had ever known. Tales of this foul fellow were told north and south. Posters warning of his rotten robberies were nailed up east and west.

ROTTEN RASCAL ROBS Without Rifle.

TINKY TAGECOACH STICK-UP.

FILTHY FELLOW STRIKES AGAIN!

Try as they might, nobody could stop Dirty Bert — no one could get close enough.

Life for Dirty Bert was as easy as rolling around in the mud. Yes sir, Dirty Bert was sitting on top of the world, till the day he decided to steal from Tallulah Tumbleweed.

Miss Tallulah ran the biggest ranch in Cactus Creek. Every Monday she rode the stagecoach back from town carrying a big chest of money to pay her ranch hands.

"This is going to be as easy as stealing candy from a baby," Bert grinned as he stood by the bridge over the creek, a cloud of flies buzzing around his head.

At high noon the stagecoach came rumbling round the bend. Wheels spinning, whip snapping, dust billowing up like storm clouds, it rolled down the road towards the bridge.

With a smirk on his face, Bert slowly raised his arms in the air and took a giant step forward. He ought not to have done that. His two muddy boots slipped out from under him. Dirty nose over dirty toes fell Bert, flying through the air like a mud pie.

"Yahoo-hoo-hoo!" With a scream he hit the water under the bridge. "Help!" Bert cried, waving his arms and kicking his feet. "I can't swim. I'm scared of water! Save me!"

Fast as a tumbleweed in a tornado, Miss Tallulah jumped out of the stagecoach. Picking up a rope, she spun it around her head and lassoed Bert as he began to sink out of sight.

Pulling him to shore like a fish, Miss Tallulah looked him up and down. "Well, bless my boots," she said, whistling. "With the dirt gone, I reckon you're about as good-looking a fellow as I've ever seen!"

"Ah, gee, Miss Tallulah," Bert blushed. "I never knew I was good at anything except being dirty."

Not long after, Miss Tallulah and Bert were married. Bertrum B. Bloomblossom (for that was Bert's real name) gave up the bandit life. He rubbed and scrubbed himself up clean as a whistle.

A few months later Bert opened the first bath-house for bandits in the Wild West. In no time he made enough money to pay back all the folks he'd robbed, with plenty left over for his favourite charity.

Bert never was arrested for being a bandit ... because nobody ever recognised him.